WITHDRAWN

Arthur's Halloween Costume

An I Can Read Book®

ARTHUR'S HALLOWEEN COSTUME

Story and Pictures by

Lillian Hoban

HarperCollins*Publishers*

HarperCollins®, 📖®, and I Can Read Book®
are trademarks of HarperCollins Publishers Inc.

Library of Congress Cataloging-in-Publication Data
Hoban, Lillian.
    Arthur's Halloween costume.

    (An I can read book)
    Summary: Arthur the chimpanzee, after worrying that
his Halloween costume won't be scary enough, wins a
prize for the most original costume in the school.
    [1. Chimpanzees—Fiction. 2. Halloween—Fiction]
I. Title. II. Series.
PZ7.H635Art 1984   [E]   83-49465
ISBN 0-06-022387-1
ISBN 0-06-022391-X (lib. bdg.)

It was the morning of Halloween.

Arthur was looking

for his schoolbooks.

Violet was packing her lunch.

She packed a chicken sandwich

and some Halloween candy.

"I am going to be a fairy queen

at the school party," she said.

"What are you going to be, Arthur?"

"I am going to be a ghost

and scare everybody,"

said Arthur.

Arthur put a sheet over his head.

He flapped his arms up and down.

"Whoo-ee! Whoo-ee!" he yelled.

"Three kids in my class

are going to be ghosts," said Violet.

"Wilma is going to be

the ghost with the most."

"That is no fair," said Arthur.

"I want to be the only ghost.

Now no one will be scared."

9

"Maybe you can be a monster,"
said Violet. "Monsters are scary."
"But I do not have
a monster costume," said Arthur.
"You can make one," said Violet.
"No I can't," said Arthur.
"I have to pack my lunch
and find my schoolbooks.
Anyway, I have nothing
to make a monster costume with."
Arthur pulled the sheet
down around his neck.

"Now you look like an angel."
said Violet.

"Fooey," said Arthur.

"I want to be a ghost."

He started to pack his lunch.

"There is hardly any chicken," he said,

"and the ketchup is almost gone."

He tried to shake some ketchup

onto his sandwich.

None came out.

He whacked the bottom of the bottle.

Splat! The ketchup plopped out

all at once.

There were big blobs of ketchup

on the sandwich,

and there were big blobs

of ketchup on Arthur's costume.

"Now what am I going to do?"
asked Arthur.

"You could make believe
it is blood," said Violet.

"Then I can't even be a ghost,"
said Arthur.

"Ghosts do not have blood."

"Yoo-hoo, Violet, can I come in?"

It was Wilma.

"I brought some

little chocolate kisses for treats,"

she said,

"and I brought a

big chocolate kiss too."

Wilma's little cousin Peter

came into the house.

He was all wrapped in silver foil.

He had a brown knit hat

pulled down over his face.

A strip of white paper was sticking

out of the top of the hat.

It said CHOCOLATE KISS.

"Doesn't he look cute?" said Wilma.

"What are you supposed to be,"

she asked Arthur,

"a vampire or something?"

"I wanted to be a ghost

and scare everybody,"

said Arthur,

"but some ketchup spilled on me."

"Maybe you should be a vampire,"

said Violet.

"Vampires are scarier than ghosts."

"Anybody can be scary," said Wilma.

"Peter wanted to be scary too,

but my big sister dressed him

like a chocolate kiss.

She says it is easy to be scary,

but it is hard to be an original."

"What is an original?" asked Violet.

"My sister says it means

you get super special ideas

that no one else has,"

said Wilma,

"like being a chocolate kiss

for Halloween."

"I never get super special ideas,"

said Arthur.

"I can't be an original."

He went to find his schoolbooks.

He found his math book, his reader,

and his spelling book.

Arthur came back into the kitchen. √

"I can not find my notebook,"

he said.

"It had all my homework in it.

Now I can't even go to the party.

My teacher said,

'No homework, no party.'

This is my worst Halloween."

"I think I saw a notebook

behind the porch," said Violet.

"It was near the trash can!"

"Near the trash can!" yelled Arthur.

"How did it get out there?"

Arthur ran outside.

He looked behind the porch.

He did not see his notebook.

He looked behind a cracked mirror

that was next to the trash can.

His notebook was not there.

Arthur lifted the lid of the can
and looked inside.

He saw an old broken broom,
a piece of shaggy brown rug,
and Violet's old doll
with its head hanging loose.

Arthur picked up the doll,

the rug, and the broom.

At the bottom of the can

he saw some paper.

He poked the paper with the broom.

27

"Arthur," called Norman.

"Are you ready for school?"

"Not yet," said Arthur.

"Why are you messing around

in the trash?" asked Norman.

"Boy, you smell like a skunk!"

"No I don't," said Arthur.

"It is this rug.

I think some tuna fish

spilled on it."

"Too bad," said Norman.

"It would make a great wig

for my tramp costume."

Norman took the rug

and put it on his head.

He looked in the mirror.

"Not bad," he said.

"Hey, that is mine," said Arthur.

"Maybe *I* can use it for a wig."

"No you can't," said Norman.

"I thought of it first."

"But it came out of my trash can,"
said Arthur.

"Well, you can not have it,"
said Norman.

"It is mine now."

Norman started to walk away.

"Give it back," yelled Arthur.

He stuck the broom
in front of Norman.

"Don't hit me

with that old broom," said Norman.

He grabbed for the broom.

Arthur held the trash can lid

in front of him.

Norman tried to yank it away.

He grabbed the doll instead.

The doll's body came away

from its head.

Norman fell backward.

"Here! Keep your old wig,"

Norman said.

"It is smelly anyway."

He jammed the rug down

on Arthur's head and walked away.

Arthur looked in the mirror.

"Hmmm," he said.

"I could be a warrior."

He held the lid in front of himself,

and lifted the broom in the air.

"This is my shield and my sword."

He swung the doll's head by its hair.

"I just killed my enemy in battle.

The ketchup is the blood.

Not a bad idea.

Maybe I am even an original!

Now I have a costume.

All I need is my notebook."

Arthur looked in the trash can again.

A big fat cat was sitting inside.

"Scat, cat!" said Arthur.

"Meow," said the cat.

It jumped to the rim of the can

and rubbed against Arthur.

Arthur pulled the paper

out of the trash can.

It was torn, and it was dirty,

and it was not his notebook.

Suddenly, Arthur felt something

scratching the back of his leg.

41

He turned to look,

but the rug fell over his eyes.

Sharp claws dug into him.

Arthur slapped at his leg

with the broom.

"Ow! Ow! Ow!" he yelled.

"Arthur," called Violet,

"stop all that yelling.

I found your notebook.

It was in your lunchbox

with an old mashed banana!"

"Yow! Yow! Yow!" Arthur yelled.

He hopped around and

waved the trash can lid in the air.

"Arthur, you stop that right now!"

called Wilma.

"You are scaring Peter

in that silly costume.

What are you anyway,

a trash collector?

You should be wearing

big work gloves.

Trash collectors always wear

big work gloves."

"Trash collector, fooey!"

yelled Arthur.

"I am *not* a trash collector!"

"He is a witch doctor!" called Violet.

"He is holding

a little shrunken head.

He is putting a spell on that cat!"

Arthur lifted the rug

from his eyes and looked down.

"Meow," said the cat.

It sniffed up at the rug

and tried to climb Arthur's leg.

"Shoo, you," said Arthur.

He shook the broom and waved

the doll's head.

"Hey! I scared Peter!

I have a scary costume!"

"Well, maybe it is scary,"

said Wilma,

"but it is not very original."

"I don't care," said Arthur.

"This is a good costume

even if I am not original.

Now let's go to school."

Arthur got his books,

his lunchbox, and his notebook.

They started off to school.

At the stoplight, Violet said,

"Arthur, the cat is following you."

"Another one is too," said Wilma.

"It must be my wig," said Arthur.

"It smells like tuna fish."

"Here come two more cats,"

said Wilma.

"Now you look like an animal trainer.

That is not very scary."

"Scat, all you cats!" yelled Arthur.

He turned around

and walked backward.

He waved the broom at the cats.

"Oh my," said the guard

at the school crossing.

"I know who you are, Arthur.

You are the Pied Piper,

the one who led all the rats

out of the village.

But you are leading cats

instead of rats!

How sweet!"

"I am not sweet!" yelled Arthur.

"I am not the Pied Piper, either.

It is not fair!

I am not scary.

I am not original.

No one even knows what I am.

Fooey!"

Arthur sat down on the curb.

A car pulled up at the stoplight.

A big dog stuck its head

out of the window.

It barked and growled.

"Are you a hobo, son?"

asked the driver.

"My dog does not like hobos."

"Grr...!" growled the dog.

"No, I am not a hobo," said Arthur.

"He must be barking at the cats,"
said the driver.

"He does not like cats, either."

"Grr...rruff!" growled the dog.

He tried to jump

through the window.

"Hisss...!" spat the fat cat.

"Hisss...meow!" Its fur stood up.

Its tail got big.

It arched its back and jumped.

It jumped right on Arthur's wig

and dug its claws in hard!

"Oh no!" yelled Arthur.

"Well, that sure is

a great costume!" said the driver.

He laughed and drove away.

"Arthur," called Wilma's big sister.

"Let me see your costume."

She got off her bike

and walked around Arthur.

58

"Wow!" she said.

"What a great idea!

That is the most original costume

I have ever seen!

Hey! Look at Arthur's costume!"

she called to the kids

in the schoolyard.

"Hey! Look at Arthur's costume!"

yelled the kids.

They all crowded around.

"Not bad," said Norman.

"What are you anyway,

the cat's meow?"

"No, he is not!"

said Wilma's big sister.

"He is The Spirit of Halloween!"

"What a splendid idea, Arthur,"
said the school principal.
"No one ever thought of that before."
He came out of the schoolyard.

"The cat can not come
into the school, Arthur,
but you certainly have my vote
for the most original costume."

"That is great," said Violet.

"You get double the treats!"

"Oh boy!" said Arthur.

"I think I am going to like

being The Spirit of Halloween!"

5/02